Happiness Is Having Friends

By Christine Economos
Illustrated by Pat Paris

Copyright © 2000 Metropolitan Teaching and Learning Company.
Published by Metropolitan Teaching and Learning Company.
Printed in the United States of America.
ISBN 1-58120-066-8

2 3 4 5 6 7 8 9 CL 03 02 01

Marta came home from school singing a song. "I'm home, Mama," she said, and put her books on the table. She got out a snack, sat down at the table, and started to eat.

"You sound happy," said Mama. "What is that song you're singing?"

"Ben and I went to the tryout for the school chorus," said Marta. "This is the song we learned. We did well. Now we'll sing with the school chorus next year."

Carlos walked in holding a basketball. He quickly took a rice cake from Marta's plate. "Carlos! Get your own," she said. "Why is your face so red?"

"I went to the tryout for the basketball team," said Carlos. "I've been playing every day. My hard work helped me do well at the tryout. The coach said I have a position on the team!"

"I'm so proud of both of you," said Mama.

After dinner, Marta and Carlos sat at the table doing their homework. Mama and Papa were in the living room talking quietly. "Papa looked very happy when he got home," Carlos said. "He must have some good news."

"Marta! Carlos!" Mama called. "Come into the living room."

"Now we'll find out why Papa is so happy," said Carlos. He pushed out his chair.

"Maybe Papa got a raise," said Marta.

Marta and Carlos went into the living room. "Your papa and I have some very big news," said Mama.

"Did you get a raise, Papa?" asked Marta.

"How did you know, Marta?" Papa asked. "Yes, I got a raise. I also got a new position. It's a position I've wanted for a long time."

"This is great," Carlos said. "Our wishes have come true! Marta made the school chorus. I made the team. And Papa got a new job and a raise!"

Carlos could see that the happiness had left Papa's face. "So what's wrong?" asked Carlos. "You should be happy, Papa."

"I am happy," said Papa. "I'm proud of you both. But changes can be hard. The new job is in a new location. Our family is going to have to move to the country."

"I don't want to move," said Marta.

"I just made the team," said Carlos. "What about all our friends? I'm not moving to a new location, Papa. I'm staying right here."

Marta was filled with sadness. A tear rolled down her face. Carlos looked at his shoes. He was proud that Papa got a new position and a raise. But Carlos was also sad. He didn't want to leave the block or his friends.

"We have to move, Carlos," said Mama. "I know it's a big change. Your friends can come and stay. We'll be living in a big house."

"I won't get to play basketball," said Carlos. "And it's all your fault."

Marta and Carlos didn't tell their friends about the move. They thought maybe Mama and Papa would not want to move after all. But the next Saturday, Mama, Papa, Carlos, and Marta drove to the new town to see the new house.

It was a pretty drive. They drove by fields filled with flowers. They saw woods and lakes. Marta and Carlos sat quietly in the back. Soon they came up to a big house.

A man met them at the door. He showed the family around the house. Marta's room looked out over a field and a stream.

Marta and Carlos walked to the stream. "Being in the country is like being on vacation," said Marta.

"Some vacation," said Carlos. "Do you see a place to play basketball? Do you see any kids? I worked hard to make the team. Now I can't play. It's all Papa's fault."

A few days later, Nina, Ben, and Marta were walking to school. "We'll get to sing songs from all over the world in chorus next year," said Ben.

"I can't be in the chorus," said Marta. "My dad has a new job. We're moving to a new location in the country."

"You're leaving the block?" asked Ben. "You can't, Marta. You're my best friend in the world."

"Mine, too," said Nina.

"It's not my fault," said Marta. "We have to move. I'm going to miss you both. You can both come and stay at our house in the country. There's a field and woods and a stream. It will be like a vacation."

"That sounds nice," said Ben. He was quiet the rest of the way to school. He was so unhappy. He wanted to tell Marta how much he would miss her. But the words would not come out.

A few weeks later, the family started packing for the move. Sara came to help Carlos pack. "Where did all this junk come from?" Carlos asked. He hauled a big box from out of the closet. "Haven't we packed enough?"

"Why don't you sell your stuff at a sidewalk stand?" said Sara with a laugh. "That way you won't have to haul it all with you."

"Very funny," said Carlos. "Been there, done that. One sidewalk stand is enough."

Mama and Marta went through Marta's books and toys. They packed some things, and gave away others. "Do you want this book?" Mama asked.

"I loved that book," said Marta. "Ben liked it, too. I think I will give it to him."

"What about this little bear?" asked Mama.

"Nina likes that bear," said Marta. "I'll give it to her. And here is a doll for Tasha."

All the kids on the block came by on moving day. A huge moving van sat in front of Marta's house. Men hauled chairs, tables, and boxes out of the house. "You can sleep over any time, Marta," said Nina.

"And you can come and stay with me, too," said Marta. "I hope you do. You too, Ben."

"The block won't be the same without you, Carlos," said Sara. Carlos could feel his tears start.

The truck was packed. It was time for Marta and Carlos to go. They hugged all their friends. Nina gave Marta a little ring. Tasha gave her a picture she had made. "You're the best friends in the world," Marta said.

Ben handed Marta a card. "This is from me," he said. Papa, Mama, Marta, and Carlos drove away. Marta and Carlos looked until they couldn't see their friends. Marta brushed the tears from her face. She opened Ben's card and read what he wrote.

Dear Marta,

Sadness is seeing you go.
Sadness is not playing with you.
Sadness is missing you.
Happiness is talking to you on the telephone.
Happiness is making cards to send you.
Happiness is going to see you.
Happiness is knowing you are my friend.

Your friend,
Ben